CAN YOU FIND SADIE?

Written by Diane Ohanesian
Illustrated by Susan Miller

To Jordan—D.O.   To my parents—S.M.

A GOLDEN BOOK • NEW YORK

Western Publishing Company, Inc., Racine, Wisconsin 53404

I need to find my puppy—
She ran away from me.
I call my puppy Sadie.
Where can that puppy be?

Can you find Sadie?

We looked in Mama's bedroom—
"Where's Sadie?" Mama said.
"I wonder if that puppy is
Beneath my great big bed?"

Can you find Sadie?

We climbed up to the attic;
I looked inside a box.
All I found were fancy hats
And piles of winter socks.

Can you find Sadie?

We hurried to the playroom;
I looked beside my bear.
Toys and games were on the floor
But Sadie wasn't there.

Can you find Sadie?

We headed for the kitchen;
I peeked behind a door.
Pots and pans were scattered on
My mama's kitchen floor.

Can you find Sadie?

We ran out to the toolshed;
I looked above a shelf.
I saw a shiny mirror there
And found someone—myself!

Can you find Sadie?

We raced out to the swing set;
I looked beneath the slide.
I found my pail and shovel but
Where did that puppy hide?

Can you find Sadie?

We rested by the sandbox,
Then something caught my eye—

I looked behind my bright green tent
And saw a tail go by.

Can you find Sadie?

I chased that tiny tickly tail,
And there in front of me,
I found my little puppy dog,
Who I was glad to see!

Can you find Sadie?